I0619673

THE CHOICE
A TRAGEDY IN THREE ACTS

———

by Hannah James Packard

*Edited and with an Introduction
by Deborah L. Halliday*

The Choice: A Tragedy.
Copyright © 2020 Deborah L. Halliday
Produced and printed
by Stillwater River Publications.
All rights reserved. Written and produced in the
United States of America. This book may not be reproduced
or sold in any form without the expressed, written
permission of the author and publisher.
Visit our website at
www.StillwaterPress.com
for more information.
First Stillwater River Publications Edition
Material herein, unless otherwise designated, was
originally published in The Choice: A Tragedy;
with other Miscellaneous Poems by Hannah J. Packard.
Boston. Leonard C. Bowles,1832:
ISBN: 978-1-952521-55-3
1 2 3 4 5 6 7 8 9 10
Written by Hannah James Packard
Published by Stillwater River Publications,
Pawtucket, RI, USA.
Image of Françoise de Cezelli portrait
photographed by Benoit Soubeyran
from Montpellier, France /
CC BY (https://creativecommons.org/licenses/by/2.0)
Back cover image:
Old map of the battle and siege of Leucata in 1637.
Image is in the public domain.
*Although this work is based on actual historical people and
events, the dialogue and specific action is a creation of the
playwright's imagination..*

.

Years roll on years, like swelling waves,

E'en so they pass and brightly shine;

No mortal eye their course can trace,

Nor find their destined resting place.

This little life—how short a time!

~ Hannah James Packard

INTRODUCTION

This work is a dramatization of actual historical events. In 1590, during the French Wars of Religion (1562-1598), the small city of Leucate, France, was under siege by allied French and Spanish Catholic forces. The event was part of more than a century of social change and upheaval brought about by the rise of Protestantism in Europe and the consequent challenge to the authority of the Holy Roman Church. Leucate, a small but strategically located fortified city less than 50 miles north of the Spanish border on the southern coast of France, was allied with Protestant forces.

Leucate's governor at the time was Jean de Boursiez, seigneur de Pantnaut de Barri. His capture during the siege and the subsequent actions of his wife, Françoise de Cezelly (1558 - 1615), are the subject of this play. After the siege France's King Henry IV named Françoise as governor of the city, to rule until her son, Hercule, was old enough to assume the title. Likely born in the late 1570s, Hercule was governor in 1637 when the city again came under attack by the Spanish. Starting out greatly outnumbered, he held the Spanish forces off long enough for large numbers of French reinforcements to arrive. The city was once again saved. Today Françoise de Cezelly is a heroine in French culture; a statue of her stands in the town of Leucate, which as of 2017 had a rapidly growing population of just under 4,500. The population in 1590 was undoubtedly much smaller.

Wars between Catholics and Protestants in Europe were not confined to the 16th and 17th centuries. Alliances based on religion and power helped shape politics and divisions that continue today. We need only look at the 20th century history of Northern Ireland to see remnants and repercussions of splits that started five centuries ago.

i

ABOUT THE AUTHOR
HANNAH J. PACKARD (1815-1831)

[Note: the text below is taken from a book of Packard's collected works privately published by her parents in 1832 after her death at the age of sixteen. It was presumably written by them.]

"Hannah James Packard, second and youngest daughter of Captain Henry R. Packard, was born in Duxbury Mass, April 15th, 1815. At a very early period she exhibited a fondness for rhyming, and long before she was old enough to use the pen, was in the habit of composing little verses and fables. At the age of seven or eight years, she taught her dolls to correspond by letter with the dolls of her sister. Some of these, it was observed, partaking doubtless of the genius of their mistress, were in the habit of composing their epistles in verse. But as no pains were taken to preserve these infantile effusions, they have all long since been lost.

"Her advantages for early education were small. Added to the faithful attentions of her parents, a few weeks attendance upon a common town-school, yearly, in summer, was her only opportunity for mental improvement. In her twelfth year, however, she was sent to a high school in her native village. At that time she was by no means remarkable for acquirements or exhibitions of talent. She was diffident and *painfully* distrustful of her own powers. Thinking herself inferior to most of her associates, she was at first reluctant to attend school, and when there, was almost afraid to speak, lest she should expose her imagined weakness and ignorance. A few words of censure or of ridicule might at that time have blighted this young flower in the bud. But it was Hannah's good fortune to fall under the care of an instructor, who, as soon as he perceived the germ of genius in his pupil, perceived also the delicate attentions necessary to swell, expand, and perfect it. She was encouraged and made conscious of her own powers; and, in a few months rose in a great measure above that painful diffidence which, so long as it lasted, would not fail to depress her spirits and retard her progress.

"For more than three years previous to her death, she had cherished a strong presentiment that she should not survive the age of sixteen; and all her plans and thoughts and actions were regulated accordingly. ...

"She continued a member of this school for three years. During that time and a few succeeding months, she had made herself acquainted with all the common and many of the higher branches of an English education, both plain and ornamental; had learned to read Spanish and French with ease and fluency, had made herself acquainted with Virgil and Cicero, and some smaller works in Latin, and had commenced the study of Italian. Her poetical compositions were mostly written during these three years, and accordingly before she was fifteen years old. Her Tragedy was commenced before she left school and completed soon after. This was nearly the last of her writings; for her eyes soon failed, and with them her general health. ...

"'From the first,' says one of her instructors, 'study was her passion, and thought was her pastime; the field of invention was her playground. In her reading, she passed by that class of books which usually engross so many years of childhood and youth, and from the first sought communion and felt sympathy with the great master spirits of our literature, Milton, Shakespeare, and Locke. I believe she truly loved and appreciated such authors as these; and a taste, natural and unaffected as it appeared to be, was one of the most striking evidences of her own superior genius. Such a taste implies genius. On the whole she was the most *spiritual* child I ever knew. She seemed all intellect and sentiment; intellect, acute, original, vigorous—sentiment, amiable, pure, ardent, and lofty.' ...

"The remains of Hannah J. Packard—the young, the ingenuous, the promising, the pure, were committed to the dust, August 11, 1831, in "the hope of a blessed resurrection." In this expectation, let the mourners of the dead be comforted, and say in her own beautiful language,

> "Earth! Take the tribute thou may'st not *keep*!
> Fold in thy bosom that faded flower:
> It shall spring again in a fairer bower,
> Where mourner may come not its blight to weep."

When Hannah was born the United States as a country was still new. Veterans of the American Revolution were still alive in her town. She knew at least one of them, and likely heard first-hand stories of the war. A visit to a former Revolutionary War barracks moved her. Patriotism and virtue were of the highest American ideals, yet there were those who doubted that women were capable of acting on principle and intellect rather than emotion. Hannah's choice of subject for her drama might well have been made precisely for that reason.

~ Deborah L. Halliday, August 2020

ABOUT THE PORTRAIT

The portrait of Hannah Packard shown here was painted by artist Cephas Giovanni Thompson (1809-1888). Thompson, son of a successful portrait painter, began his career in Massachusetts in 1827 when he was just eighteen. This was likely one of his earliest commissions; Hannah was twelve in 1827, and the young girl in this picture looks to be not much older than that. Thompson went on to become a renowned artist. Today his work is found in New York's Metropolitan Museum of Art, the National Portrait Gallery, the Boston Athenaeum, and the Boston Museum of Fine Arts. This portrait of Hannah was copied for lithography by "L.R.S." The lithograph was produced in 1832 for inclusion in Hannah's book by Pendleton's in Boston, established in 1825 as one of the first lithography studios in the United States.

For many years this portrait of Hannah was sold and re-sold into private collections, unidentified or misidentified. Inquiries begun in the 2010s resulted in the portrait being located and acquired in 2017 by the Duxbury Historical Society where it now hangs.

Françoise de Cezelli.
1558 - 1615.

DRAMATIS PERSONAE.

Barri – Governor of Leucate,* taken prisoner by its besiegers.

Hercules – His son

Francoli – An officer of Leucate

Bernis – A Protestant Priest of Leucate

Gerardo – A Spanish commander of The League

Le Comte – A French Commander of The League

Constanza – Wife of Barri

Genevra – Sister of Barri

Citizens, Soldiers, &tc.

* Pronounced in three syllables: Leu-ca-te.

The Scene:
The City of Leucate [France] and the Camp before it.

The Time:
During the War of the League in 1590.

THE CHOICE
A TRAGEDY

* * * * * * * *

ACT I.

[In the first scene we find Le Comte, head of the French forces, in his tent expressing his frustration at the length of the siege. He is bored, and he states his intention—as he does throughout this scene—to stop waiting and instead take direct action. His ally Gerardo, head of the Spanish forces, enters. Le Comte is jealous that Gerardo has captured Barri, Governor of the city under siege; Le Comte had intended that prize for himself. He accepts when Gerardo offers to turn the prisoner over to him as a sign of alliance and goodwill. They have Barri brought before them, and Le Comte reveals his plan to barter Barri's life for the city. Gerardo objects to the plan as dishonorable, unnecessary, and likely to backfire, creating more partisan zeal among the citizens.- DLH.]

Scene I: *A tent in the Camp.*

Enter Le Comte, pacing the tent.

Le Comte: Yes, two whole tedious months have passed, and still I linger here? Could I have thought or dreamt of this before my honor was engaged as it is now, to finish ere I pause, yon walls had never mocked me thus; nor I had

1

ever planted 'neath their fortresses my Holy
Cross, which now I must support.

Gerardo too! That it has been for *him* to win
the only prize there has been won through
this whole ill-starred, soul-corroding siege;
that he shall take this Barri, when I've
owned— even to himself have owned—that
't was my wish, next to subduing this eter-
nal city, to make its master captive so at
least I might possess a trophy of the prow-
ess which I have wasted here, if nothing
more. Oh it is irksome even to think of it!
They say, too, that Constanza has returned,
to act another Barri; and her words have
been a charm to turn the citizens' fears to
boldness all at once. But I will prove which
is the most, Barri or woman, in her. I've
heard, indeed, uncommon shouts today,
and cheers like sounds of welcome or of joy.
Well let them shout—it will be my turn next!
It shall be! By the Holy Mass, I've borne my
penance well. Two months! Two stupid
months! Not the Pope himself should doom
a third.

Enter Gerardo

Le Comte:	Gerardo!
Gerardo:	Wilt thou suffer me to interrupt thy musings with my words?

Le Comte:	Enter! Thou art a privileged visitor; even my solitude is free for thee.
	(Aside): Or so thou mak'st it with thy liberties.
	But how goes the big world! And soldiers' hopes? Sleeps yon vain dreamer yet?
Gerardo:	What meanest thou? The City? No – it wakes! Aye, gloriously; as noble natures wake when they have fallen a moment from their height, more noble still.
Le Comte:	Dost thou confirm the rumor then that this Constanza has returned?
Gerardo:	Yes, and 't is said, the flag that waver'd on the *soldiers'* wall, a *woman's* hand has fastened there secure.
Le Comte:	We will go shake it presently, and find how long a woman's hand can hold it there. But may I ask if there be aught of moment this visit would imply?
Gerardo:	It is of Barri, the captive Governor, I would speak with thee.
Le Comte:	Ah, yes! He is thy pris'ner!

Gerardo: And he is a noble one. I would the chance of
                  war had placed him on our side, so he had
                  been a hero.

Le Comte: Ha! Dost thou? I like him little. If I may
                  speak of what concerns me not, his haughty
                  port has more the Gov'nor still than fits his
                  present state.

Gerard: I would not have his soul be mine because
                  his body is.

Le Comte: I would not have his manner taunt me so,
                  with its proud quietness. Prison and Pride!
                  The terms do not agree, yet he is pleased to
                  make their contrast stronger in himself.
                  That spirit which he bears should learn to
                  wear less haughtily its chain, were I to say.
                  But I have drawn thee from thy purpose;
                  what is it thou would'st have with me of
                  him?

Gerardo: Acceptance of him, as a warrior's gift—an
                  hostage, emblem of our amity. Permit me to
                  present this token then, to prove that War
                  itself but seals our peace more firmly.

Le Comte: *(Aside)*: Must he rival me in all? Even in
                  gifts? Yet 't is a welcome gift, most wel-
                  come.

Shall I then usurp thy praise as though I had taken Barri, and not thou? No! keep the palm thou hast so well acquired.

Gerardo.   Think not of that; it has been indeed my chance to win, and therefore would I now entrust my prize to him who best can guard it. Though the gift be small at least the motive may enhance its value. 'T is not alone in hollow compliment I proffer it, but earnestly, most earnestly, for thus I would devote me to our Holy Cause and banish every selfish spring of action from what I do for common benefit.

Le Comte.   Then I receive what may not be refused, and hold myself in debt for courtesy like this;

              (Aside). a debt of *words* I would infer, and that's now paid.

But where is he, this Barri, Leucate's plumeless Governor?

Gerardo.   I will send for him, and hasten to present him to thee. Here, Obis!

              Enter Attendant.

Attendant.   I await my chief's commands.

Gerard.   Go bring the prisoner Barri hither to us.

Attendant: My Lord, I humbly will fulfill thy bidding.

Exit Attendant.

Le Comte: Ay, the insulter is ours at last, the victim of his own wiles! Said I not, Gerardo, the Holy Crucifix would triumph still? And it shall be the sign of its own victory. Our enemies shall kneel and kiss this cross, ere they may ask for mercy.

Gerardo: Some, I fear, will not find mercy then.

Le Comte: No, not with me, unless on my conditions.

Gerardo: That word has sealed Barri's fate; for he would look on death—ay, kiss the sword which should unseal the fount of his heart's vital blood—rather than this.

Le Comte: Well then, we have a talisman to prove his hardiness, or rather to disprove it. There is a power in death to humble pride, so I have heard, and Barri may evince.

Gerardo: Evince! Surely thou would'st not tempt thy prisoner? I thought there was a higher nature in thee!

Le Comte: Well let us speak of that which deeper now concerns us than a prisoner's destiny. 'T is

certain, then, this rumored warrioress' return?

Gerardo.   Most certain; is it not time that we should
give her welcome suited to her guise?

Le Comte.   Ay—but she's Barri's other self, 't is said,
and comes to bolden their faint hearts.

Gerardo.   I'm glad if it be so indeed—our victory will
be prouder.

Le Comte.   So am I; yet do I doubt of any swift success.
Another moon and we perhaps might win
some second bravo, but I am not disposed
ten years should prove my patience 'gainst
this modern Troy. Two months have well
sufficed.

Gerardo.   Whither tend thy strange doubts! Surely
thou would'st not now forsake this siege?

Le Comte.   No, but I would pursue it, finish it at once.
I would rush forward, not crawl thus, pace
after pace, month after month, as we have
done. Thou art so slow and circumspect! I
would *do* something, though it were but
done to be undone the moment afterwards.

Gerardo.   If I'm too slow, thou art as much too quick;
if I'm too circumspect, thou art too careless.
Let us then each correct our special faults,
one by the other. But it is not sweet to be

7

reminded of our frailties, even by friends; and I would only caution thee of thy quick spirit, not impute a blame to its free, natural wanderings. Now no more of this. Here comes the prisoner.

Enter Barri, with Guards.

Gerardo: Guards, retire and wait without till you are called again.

Exeunt Guards.

Le Comte, behold thy captive!

Barri: *(Aside):* Le Comte's captive! My very chains are bartered!

Le Comte: I behold him, and thank thee for a sight so sweet to me—the Holy Cross triumphant over its foes.

(To Barri): Approach yet nearer. Let me view thee well; for I would see if thou hast not the mark of Cain upon thee, for thy heresy. Surely thou hast, or something blacker still: *he* killed a brother in his ignorance of death; *thou* wagest war upon thy brothers!

Barri: Yes, in defense, and in my knowledge of the truth.

8

Le Comte: Ha! Dost thou scoff me to my face? But do not in thy show of scorn forget that my hand has the power of Atropos to cut thy tiny thread—or dost thou think thou canst meet death as haughtily and fierce?

Barri: Death! 'T were the proudest laurel I could win! Could I meet death? Ay! and I challenge thee, thou who hast dared insult me with doubt! Yet I forget; I am thy prisoner now, and chained to insult. I should learn to bear in silence. But thou *can'st* not chain my thoughts.

Gerardo: Thou should'st have been a Spaniard for thy spirit!

Le Comte: And thou may'st be a papist for thy soul.

Barri: I am content to be the prisoner Barri, fortune's blown bubble that your breaths would break.

Le Comte: 'Tis well thy wishes are so limited. Yes, well for thee; the worm should not essay to reach the eagle's height. Yet there is hope even for the worm; it may avoid the step whose crush is death.

Then are thy hopes all crushed? A moment since thou would'st have challenged me! Now thou art content, forsooth, to be my prisoner! Yet thou, even *thou* may'st hope—

vile as thou art! Vile as thou hast been! For our Holy Church turns not from penitents. Thou may'st return, confess thy guilt, even be forgiven still, as madmen are forgiven for the things they did in their delirium, if thou wilt. Behold this pledge of mercy! *(Lifts a cross).* I extend even to thy stained lips its holy touch; kiss this, and thou art free! Not from our power alone, which bows to *this* and owns itself nothing, but from the power of error over thy higher part!

Barri.   Ay, that's beyond thy reach! Thou hast said well; there is a higher part, far, far above thy bribings; though thou dost besiege it, like yon walls, its sanctuary never—no never— shall my honor yield. And is it honor in thee to seduce, if I might be seduced? Call me not vile! Art thou not vilest to insult thy victim? To offer what it were vileness to accept? But thou may'st offer; I can still deny. Not even *thou* can'st force thy will on me! Thou can'st but only use thy utmost power of earth on me, and what is that? The means soonest to set me free from earthly power! Go on, insult me as thou wilt; for I can answer, and I will not smooth my speech, no more than I would blunt my weapon's point if I might meet thee in the battle field, and sign thee for the mark of its direction.

Le Comte.   Who speaks of insult? Am not I insulted? Braved, bearded?

Gerardo.   Le Comte, hold! Is this thy promise? Is this,
               indeed thy honor? Deem'st thou thus to
               hasten victory? We did not come to form
               new partisans, but conquer cities. Silence!
               For shame at least, if not for else!

Le Comte.   Thou too, Gerardo? Dost thou countenance
               yon thing? Yet I forget; such heroism ac-
               cords with thee, but 'tis not of *my* nature;
               and thou, methinks, should know its wind-
               ings well enough to be more cautious how
               thou thwarts them.

               But take thy gift again, if thou must be my
               arbiter in using it; I want no gifts when I
               must have the giver too to counsel me, and
               never be released from the vast obligation of
               the debt. Not I!

Gerardo.   Le Comte, dost thou insult me too? But I ex-
               cuse thee, for I know thy nature, as thou
               hast said, too well to hope for else than in-
               sult in it anger. But restrain this sudden
               passion; dost thou rule an army, and can'st
               thou not govern thine own words?

Le Comte.   Right, right! I own myself in fault. Yet for-
               give; for thou, who fail'st in nothing, can'st
               forgive as well as censure, and thou fail'st
               not there. But I am little versed in keeping
               peace, much less in asking it, as thou
               may'st deem. The battle, not the camp, were

made for me, and I am ruffled with the tedi-
ousness of this. I've lingered in it much too
long; I cannot brook such separate, petty
siege! I would not seek the hare in his hid
covert, while others trace the stag!

Gerardo.   What would'st thou do? Or what has hap-
pened thus to ruffle thee? For thou, indeed,
art strangely moved.

Le Comte.   Oh nothing! Nothing but thought, and that
might ruffle Satan if he could pause in his
demonic task to think. I've passed the
bound of all endurance. My patience is ex-
hausted, spent, worn out. I've thought and
thought. Now I will act! And I will be revenged for this delay at least, though it is
past redeeming now. There is one present
who shall answer all; one who has even
dared me to exert my power on him, and he
shall find I can. Ay, and I will: his city or his
Lord! My camp shall be within yon stirring
walls, or he shall be their ransom!

Gerardo.   Art thou mad? Or art thou frightened by a
woman's voice, who bids her knights defend
her?

Le Comte.   Thou hast said what would have called my
blood, another time, in hasty rushings; but
no matter now— I will return the compliment of pardon. I am not mad nor frighted,
Don Gerardo, but I'm resolved; resolved to

do at once what months have not accomplished yet. Thy gift comes in good time to second my intent, for which I'm doubly debtor.

Gerardo: Le Comte, pause! Dost thou indeed mean as thou say'st?

Le Comte: 'Tis not my habit to speak lightly. Yes, I mean—and by our Holy League I *swear*—

Gerardo: Swear not – till I may be the partner of thine oath, as I am in the cause by which thou tak'st it.

Le Comte: Well then, I say, affirm, declare—and mark! I *mean* withal, the governor or the governed, the palace or the thing that had a palace, Barri or Barri's city, shall be mine. Speak I not plainly? Can'st thou not even yet conceive my purpose?

Gerardo: No! I will not think thou mean'st aught else than Le Comte should intend.

Le Comte: I mean to end this siege! Let Barri choose between himself and what was his!

Barri: Ay! let me choose; turn him not—let him prove me! Doubt'st thou I can stand his proof? Oh might it be indeed for me to choose between my city's fall and my own single death, my city's honor or my slight pain—how soon the choice were made!

Le Comte: Rather how soon 'twere thought, or said, or dreamt—*made* is a nearer test! But let that pass. Thou dost not know yon walls contain a treasure more precious than the rubies of the East that monarchs fought for—and as dangerous perhaps to its possessor—and to thy high vaunting it may be too hard a trial. Constanza, thy Constanza, has returned. Returned to thee! Heaven and she know how. And shall she coo amid yon towers in vain? Wilt thou forsake her in this doubtful siege, to die from very spite? When thou might'st be the one to ransom her?

Barri: Ay, by disgracing her and myself?

Le Comte: Rather by saving both from double death!

Gerardo: Le Comte, no more of this, if thou would'st have me own thee Le Comte still. Think'st thou; this woman, if she has the heart of woman in her, will not she sooner faint at the first burst of our artillery than mail her fears when soldiers' nerve grow weak? Trust me, we're nearer conquest now than ever.

Le Comte: We might be!

Gerardo: We may be! Prove if my words are true or not; and be the forfeit mine if they are false!

14

Let us not our own selves destroy the only trophy of our toils, and for no purpose.

Le Comte: Well, I yield to thee Gerardo, as the elder and the wiser;

(Aside): in self-esteem, at least, and that's thy standard.

Guards, there!

Enter Guards

Lead Barri to his tent again, and keep your stations by him closely. Prisoner, Farewell! and thank Gerardo for thy safety.

Barri: I owe my safety to a higher Will than his or thine; and I will only thank Him who has given it, and who has the power to make it endless, if He please. Farewell! God judge between us and support his cause!

Exit Barri, Guarded.

Le Comte: He's gone! The viper! But his sting will turn upon himself.

Gerardo: Divert thy thoughts from him; 'tis time that we salute this lady-chief.

Le Comte: As never knight before saluted her. I doubt she might not choose such serenade.

Gerardo: It is not at her option to decide; but let us
               go prepare the instruments!

                        Exeunt.

[In Scene II Constanza has just returned home, not yet knowing whether her husband, child, and sister-in-law are still alive. Francoli assures her that they are, but that her husband is in danger. He urges her to hide any display of emotion so that the citizens and soldiers of Leucate will take courage from her resolve and see in her the leader they so desperately need. Genevra, Barri's sister, enters with Hercules, son of Constanza and Barri. Genevra is unable to control her expression of fear and grief, even though Contanza and Bernis, the priest, urge her to do so. - DLH.]

Scene II: *A hall in the palace of Barri.*

Enter Constanza and Francoli.

Constanza: Sweet home! My home and his! Ah, now I feel all that I could not realize before! Yes, he is lost indeed! My widowed heart, there is no home for thee.

(to Francoli): Oh teach me now the firmness I have taught to bolder nerves, if that thou say'st be true. Teach me the hope that I have given to others, but to make mine own despair more desperate.

Francoli: Are there, then, none left to welcome thy re-
                turn even yet? No other loved ones still?

Constanza: Where is that friend, who ever was the first
                to welcome me? But tell me, Oh! What of my
                Hercules? My boy, my all of Barri that is
                left? Is he yet left to me? Or have they taken
                this last one too? Speak! Is he well and safe?
                Oh answer, quickly answer! That alone may
                soothe me now, to know my child is safe.

Francoli: Thy child is safe, and if there be a might in
                firm resolve to do the thing it means, his fa-
                ther shall be so.

Constanza: My darling boy! Unmindful yet of ill! He can-
                not know his father's grief, his mother's ag-
                ony. And may he not! He shall remain to me
                a sunbeam in the tempest. All around, how
                dark—how beautiful that one bright spot!
                But of Genevra; is she left me still? Have I a
                sister and a child indeed?

Francoli: Yes, and forget not that thou hast, too, souls
                which vibrate to thy touch. Be thou firm,
                and they are armed and adamant; but yield
                to feelings that flow forth so naturally – 'tis
                hard to check them, yet they must be
                checked—and all of man in them yields too.

18

Constanza: What need for me then to be firm, since thou
                 hast said that all are weak but me? Who
                 calls those brave, whose courage wavers at
                 a woman's voice? If I must steel my heart to
                 strengthen theirs—

Francoli: Then Barri may be saved!

Constanza: Ah yes! I feel the force of thy reproof. I
                 should be calm; I must be, can be, and I will!
                 There is a strength in love even to restrain
                 itself, and I will prove it. Deep, deep in my
                 soul, too far for grosser thought to pene-
                 trate, shall be this silent sorrow—sacred
                 there, my grief shall be mine own, my cher-
                 ished treasure. Nought but the spirits of my
                 ancestors may be for other eyes to look
                 upon. Yes, yes, I can be firm! For Barri's
                 sake I can be anything. I can even seem that
                 which I am not.

Francoli: Be but what thou seem'st—a happy omen
                 sent to reassure our failing hopes. Now we
                 are strong again! Thou see'st the visible
                 change thy words have caused, from lowest
                 despair to highest confidence, through all
                 our garrison. And let me be the first to speak
                 a city's gratitude for this so opportune

encouragement. But citizens' hearts and soldiers' are not things to trust too far; let not their fears relapse! That were more dangerous even than what has been. And pardon me this freedom, for thou knowest how much of zeal thy fortitude inspires, and how much his safety, in whose place thou are, rests on devoted zeal.

Constanza: I know it all! And thank thee for thy words which have revived Cezelli's spirit in me. Tender thoughts and softer feelings I have cherished; now, the time to weep has passed. Be done with such! The universal care should claim us now, the universal effort; and of that, (so I may better know if there indeed be any cause for effort) I would ask one simple question; simply answer me. Might thou be free to choose thy part, unbound by all which binds thee now, what were that choice?

Francoli: Were I to choose for safety on which side my fortunes should embark, it would be this! Were I to choose for loyalty my side, it would be this! And might my choice be made the dictate of the still small voice alone, it would be this! Safety and loyalty and conscience fight for us, and Doubt is not admitted to their counsels. As my soul reveres the truth, so have my words declared it; but would'st thou now my further services? Or would thy musings rather be alone, and grant me leave of absence? I but wait to know and do thy pleasure.

Constanza: Go then now, Francoli, with my grateful approbation. Thy services are written on my soul, not even grief shall blot their memory thence! Go; do Francoli's part; that is enough. And now farewell.

Exit Francoli.

Constanza: *(solo)*: My husband, and my sister, and my boy! My soul is with them all! Yet I am here, alone, away from all. Oh let me haste to clasp those treasures which I still may clasp to this poor trembling heart. Hark! heard I not that little well-known step upon the stair, as light as when it leaped in happier days to seek a father's presence?

Enter Genevra and Hercules

Yes! My child! Come, come, thou hast a mother left thee yet!

Hercules:	*(running to Constanza)*: Mamma! My dear mamma! How very glad I am to see thee! For I almost thought thou never would'st come back again.
Constanza:	Genevra! Thou too! Ah, all but one!
Genevra:	Yes, all but one. And that one all! Oh when we parted last who could have dreamed of this, of such a meeting? To part in smiles and only meet to mourn!
Constanza:	Yet do not yield thus to such gloomy fears; try, try to be more firm.
Genevra:	More firm, indeed! No, let me weep! Sure I may weep at least! Yes, that allowance even the captive claims; it is the common privilege of grief! They cannot chain her tears, no more than they could number mine! Oh "try to be more firm" – make *thou* the trial. Let me weep alone!
Constanza:	Say not alone; thou hast the sympathy of tears at least; thou hast the sympathy of a crushed heart, still in its wretchedness! Yet, dear Genevra, wilt thou not at least for my sake be more calm? And for thine own, and for his sake for whom even thy gay spirit has

learned what sadness is? I too could yield to all the dark thoughts which despair might dream! And I *have* yielded, and my heart still yields to feelings natural to its woman- ish temper; but my *soul* shall not yield! No, I have known Barri too long to love him self- ishly. What are our griefs, what our most anxious fears, to the so many griefs, so many fears, of all the citizens? They look to us for firmness and support; shall they look in vain to Barri's wife, or Barri's sister?

Genevra: And do they look to us for confidence? We who must feel the most, must we be the ones to bear the most? Must we seem calm? Dissemble even sorrow? Shall we not even have grief's indulgence? Tears at least? But break not yet, my heart! Thou canst not have much longer to endure!

Constanza: And break not yet *my* heart! Thou must en- dure! Oh think of me; should not my sorrow even be more than thine? Yet I must bear it all, and hide it all! I may not even weep, lest I should shake the soldiers' firmness with my tears. But if it is for Barri, what can I not bear? At least I will not yield. My heart in- deed may break beneath its torture of restraint, but I will stretch it to the farthest nerve of suffering first!

Genevra: I would, I could, endure all, everything but this, with fortitude. But I have loved him too devotedly to hush one cry, even for a city's sake! What is a city? Is not Barri more than all the world to me? And shall I know his precious safety hazarded and seem still to be firm because my looks are watched by cowards, whose faint hearts are moved to fear to see me yield to natural feeling? No! *Thou* mayst be calm, I cannot, would not be.

Constanza: Yet hear me, hear! Is it not for Barri's sake that I would have thee so? His precious safety, his city's honor; all, thou knowest, depends on this last effort, and a *breath* might move Leucate's wavering firmness. Even thy tears, so frail has loyalty become, Genevra! Think not my soul unfeeling as my words; that, that can feel! But thy grief needs no aid from mine!

Genevra: O do not check one sigh for me! I had rather hear his name, though breathed in mournfulness, than aught beside. Still speak of him, and I will listen.

Constanza:	It is not well that we should still increase each other's doubts by telling them. No, let us weep alone, endure together! It is for Barri's sake!

Enter Bernis

Bernis! Thou art most welcome!

Bernis:	Rather I should welcome thee; *thou* art indeed most welcome. At least Leucate proves how thou art welcomed! Confidence comes with thee, and Hope and Will which most have failed before are firmest now. And soldiers look on thee and learn to be soldiers indeed, who have been baser things. Thou hast performed a hero's part today, and heroes wake, as kindred, at thy coming.

Constanza:	And thou hast been the hero in mine absence. Said I the hero? The preserver, rather! Thou hast indeed preserved life, honor, friends—all that is still mine own I owe to thee! But one, alas; thy care has failed for one, dearer I'd almost said, dearer than all. And that one, tell me now the real truth of him; shall I ever welcome him back to his royal home again?

Bernis: We know not, we may not say, what shall
                be; but we trust, and we have trusted, and
                beholding thee our trust increases—for
                there is a charm, a heavenly charm which
                angels might employ, bound to thy words as
                though some spirit breathed upon them
                with the breath of prophecy to tell our trust
                of good. Thou who hast ever brought happi-
                ness before, art now deemed but the mes-
                senger of former joy to come again—such is
                our fond belief. We hoped in doubt, but now
                we hope in trust.

Genevra: O that we had a mirror for our hopes, a little
                fairy gift such as we read of in ancient tales;
                a magic oracle where one side would reflect
                our every wish, and all incumbent on our-
                selves would be to turn the glass, and find
                them realized!

Bernis: One gift we have, better than fairy gift,
                where we may learn not what our wishes are
                (for that, unaided, we can find too oft) but
                what they should be. Then we turn the page
                and read that there is One who hears our
                prayers and answers them in mercy, though
                too high and infinite in his almighty pur-
                pose for our weak finite minds to compre-
                hend always, yet always merciful; the more,

perhaps, the less our senses can compass His boundless goodness, all too vast for us! And we should thank Him, even when the weight of woe is heaviest on us, that His hand has still preserved us from a bitterer grief.

Genevra: Yes, father, I can listen to thy words, and know that all thou sayest should be so; but ah! Not even thou canst guide my heart and make it learn to beat less audibly. Joy dwells unclouded there, or sunless grief, the Northern Winter, or the Equator's heat. Calmness and patience were not made for me! The avalanche should be my covering; I would be crushed at once!

Bernis: But would'st thou not avert the avalanche from others' heads?

Genevra: Ah yes! Thou hast reproved me with just cause; I do forget of others in myself, when I should not remember self for them. Constanza! Wilt thou then forgive me that I still keep harping on that tenderest string, when otherwise perhaps its tone were hushed?

Constanza: Hushed? Never! No, Genevra, never be it
                hushed for me! But thou—I would not have
                thee too imbibe the woe thou can'st not aid.

Genevra: O thou art generous and would'st not have
                a flower be withered by thy sorrow's breath.
                But I am so absorbed in my one thought, I
                love my brother so, I cannot think, I cannot
                speak, of anything but him.

Constanza: I wish thee not—it is the dearest subject and
                the most grateful. Yet I would not have
                doubt mingle with our holy trust for him.
                His fate is with a Higher Power than ours,
                and on that power we will, we *do* rely. Our
                love is pure; it should be confident, for in-
                nocence is ever confident.

Genevra: O I am confident, whatever be the sequel of
                his fate, it will be right. Yet how, how could
                I know of what I dread but that my earthly
                part would bear me down? And though I
                must submit, how heavily my heart would
                bear the weight of its submission!

Bernis: But it is right that we should ever hope,
                even though our hope be almost foolish-
                ness. What were even heaven without? And
                he whose grief is inconsolable despair but

28

shows that his own pleasure was his dearest life, and when that failed, he would not live for else.

But I will not further interrupt you. I know that sorrow seeks no witnesses to its free gushings, and I will not be a check upon you when I may not aid. But do not let the o'erflowing of your grief be marked by vulgar eyes lest they construe, according to their lower feelings, yours, and deem that fear alone could move you thus. And now farewell. The trying moment comes when woman's heart grows faint.

Genevra: What dost thou say? Is it the time for blood to flow again? Is there any show of preparation, as if they would come for further victims soon?

Bernis: There is indeed. But think upon our Holy Cause and trust, and fear not! There is a mightier aid on our side than numbered hosts. Hast thou not often read of armies, shouting in their vaunted strength, fallen ere that strength was proved, beneath the blow which none can parry? And is not that same protector of the weak our guardian too? Yes, if we do believe in earnestness, and cherish not a doubt though scarcely known to our most secret thoughts, we shall at last find our reward.

Constanza: Yes father! But thou knowest that there are times when the full burdened heart, surcharged by earth, may not be raised above its narrowness—and now mine will be linked to earthly thoughts. It must!

Bernis: An even on earth our self restraint will find its recompense in its own memory, if is nothing else.

Constanza: Well we will try to do as thou hast said.

Bernis: Then I depart; remember there is One who looks upon the weak, for their support, and on the sorrowful, to comfort them.

Constanza: Adieu! And may thy words be realized!

Genevra: May they indeed! That prayer was mine, Constanza!

Constanza: Our prayers shall be together. He has said, in whose blest name we offer them, that aught agreed upon and asked in supplication by two or three assembled in that

name—a common prayer, which mingles
different souls in high commune beyond the
thoughts of earth—that shall be granted to
their mutual wish!

Genevra: Then if sincerity finds its reward in what it
seeks, ours must be regarded. But come, let
us retire awhile, Constanza; sure thou must
need repose.

Constanza: Oh no; I rest not, but I will go with thee.
Come then my boy; my little Barri whom I
still possess!

Exeunt omnes.

* * * * * * * *

ACT II.

[Scene I opens with Francoli leading the citizens of Leucate
toward what will be the battle ground in front of the palace.
They stop to pay homage to Constanza and ask her for
words of encouragement. This she gives them, along with
her scarf which will be their banner and rallying point in
battle. - DLH]

Scene I: *Space before the Palace of Barri.*

*Enter Francoli and citizens on their march
towards the ramparts.
They stop before the palace.*

1st *Citizen*:   Here let us pause and play that martial tune
                which Barri loved to well.

2nd *Citizen*:   It would but be reminding her of grief; no,
                let us go and prove that we are Barri's fol-
                lower!

1st *Citizen:*   Francoli is our leader—let him say which
                counsel he approves.

33

Francolī: Then we will do as thou proposed—it will not long defer, and sure we owe this compliment, at least, to one who has been all but Barri to us.

Citizens: Yes, yes—we'll pay this compliment to her!

They play a martial symphony.

Enter Constanza from the palace.

Citizens: *(shout)*: God save our noble mistress! And restore our noble master soon!

Constanza: And God preserve his loyal citizens to welcome him!

Francolī: Such is thy greeting—but thy foes shall have a rougher one, ere long.

3rd Citizen: Ay, and they should! 'Tis time that we retort on our side too, not suffer and be still, as we have done.

Constanza: I thank you for this spirit; 'tis an earnest of what your deeds will be.

4th Citizen: Of what they must be, with so bright stimulations to excite our highest bravery.

34

Constanza: And you have the will to *be* excited—that is
                 more than all!

2ⁿᵈ Citizen: *(to Francoli)*: Hear'st thou those sounds? We
                 must not linger here.

5ᵗʰ Citizen: On, on! The rampart is the scene for us!

1ˢᵗ Citizen: But let us hear thy parting word before we
                 rush, perhaps to part with words of earth
                 forever. Thou, whose voice has been the sig-
                 nal to rouse our flagging firmness!

Constanza: I can say but what your hearts have said
                 and felt already. I can but add my voice to
                 all the prayers of *all* who pray now if they
                 ever will. But I will add it, if it may avail,
                 most grateful that your loyalty has left one
                 thing for me to do of benefit. And if you thus
                 will seek my words before the contest, may
                 it be for me the first to hail you *victors* when
                 the strife is over to which your zeal would
                 haste. Till then, farewell. Farewell indeed!
                 My soul breathes out that prayer in earnest-
                 ness. Think, should the foe advance with
                 Herculean strength, think on the cause for
                 which you struggle and a might will come to
                 arm your nerveless frames against the force
                 of those whose power is strengthened by the

chance of earthly fortune only, and whose war is leagued in vice against a holier strife! This is your native city! It has seen your birth, and it may look upon your death, but shall it see you yield to else than death? No, never! It has been the sacred shrine of all your happiness or misery. You would not mar the memory of the first, and misery loves to linger near the spot of its sad lamentations, or to bury itself beneath the sod of buried joy.

Your friends are here, your home, your all is here. Yet one is absent! Wish you his return? Then seek, as warriors seek what they would have! But why do I repeat all this to you, already eager to remove the brand of fear from your fair names? It is not well that I should thus seem almost to insult with woman's voice a soldier's spirit more. Forgive me that I spoke to you so long of what you know full well. And now we part. Go—I will not restrain your eagerness with further words. Go, and God speed your cause!

Citizens: We go to do as thou hast said!

Francoli: *(to Constanza)*: Yet I would still ask one boon of thee.

Constanza: Name it, and it is granted.

Francoli: Would'st thou lend thy scarf? It is the fittest banner we should bear, who owes to thee almost the power to bear it.

Constanza: Thou hast it; may it be a happy sign! Oh could I charm it with some gifted word of more than mortal might! But no; my prayers shall be its only dower—take this, and them. *(Gives him the scarf.)*

Francoli: Once more, my thanks. And now to show their truth!

                 (To the citizens): This is your banner! On! It is the emblem of your returning valor; shame it not! For Barri—on!

                 (Exeunt Francoli and Citizens)

Constanza: For Barri! Oh my heart, support thine anguish and be still!

                 (Exit into the palace)

[In Scene II Genevra and Constanza wait in the palace for word of the battle, the sounds of which they can hear below. Bernis comes to give them an update and to reassure them, asking them to trust in God. Francoli arrives to ask Bernis to come lend his hand on the battlefield; Constanza agrees, and Bernis goes. After a time Bernis returns to deliver the good news that the enemy is in retreat. All remain anxious, however, and each seeks out a place of solitude in which to await more news. - DLH]

Scene II: *Hall in the Palace, as before.*

Enter Genevra and Hercules.

Hercules: Dear aunt! Wilt thou not answer? Has papa
                  returned?

Genevra: O no, my love. Might I but know that he
                  would ev— but thou may'st leave me now.

                  (Exit Hercules)

                  (*solo*): Go, sport and joy in the free buoyancy
                  of thy young heart; forget thou ever had'st a
                  father. Trust to me for memory! Thou art too
                  young for sorrow, and the world is new to
                  thee, and seems all happiness. But there
                  are many griefs thy waning years must
                  learn, fair boy! Thou need'st not seek them

38

yet. It will be time enough when they will come unasked, unsought, to thee—the gifts of knowledge.

But it is ever thus. We will not learn from others' sad experience or believe their warnings of our fate till we have proved, ourselves, by knowing, all they felt before. Knowing the world! That is to know ourselves upon a larger scale and learn to be a portion of the wretched things around.

Yet all are not mere worldlings! I have felt that they are not, and that may prove my grief; for if he were more like the common mass of cold but kindred earth, I had not loved so well, or felt, so deeply felt, his loss. But now I must; should I not feel it? yet they say I should be calm, and hoard my grief with miserly care, as though I would belie it, as misers to possession of their wealth. But that would be mere mockery; worse than mockery! I could not seem resigned! I should but show myself unfeeling.

Enter Constanza.

Ah, Constanza! What, what have we more to suffer?

Constanza: Nerve thee now! Trust in the God of battles
              and be firm. The word is given—the soldiers
              have gone forth. All is ready but this poor
              weak heart, and this too shall be. Hark! did
              I not hear? Yes, there it is—the voice of mor-
              tal hate! The thunder that they cannot rule
              in heaven they mock on earth, with more in-
              human aim. I did not deem—it might be
              thoughtlessness, for my thoughts wander
              strangely—but I deemed not so soon the
              fiendish work would be begun.

Genevra: Ah, those sounds are familiar to my ear!
              Thou hast to use thyself to them, Con-
              stanza, if thou would'st be of us. Alas, my
              brother! He hears those sounds too, but
              they are to him only a higher degree of mis-
              ery, for I know that his high spirit ill can
              brook a prisoner's helplessness while others
              strive for his sake, in the cause which
              should be his. I know all the quick thoughts
              that come and go o'er his mind's surface,
              and the deeper ones that linger in its
              depths. Yes, I can feel with Barri, being the
              twin to all the frailties which I could never
              find in him, or if I did, I should but love him
              dearer by the increase of our alliance
              thence; and for his virtues, if I have any, 'tis

because he is so virtuous, and I have learned to love virtue by loving him, its noblest boast. Methinks, before, I never realized the half his merits; and now that they are the farthest from my grasp, they seem to be the brightest, like the Sun which ever is most beautiful at setting.

Enter Bernis.

Constanza: Bernis! Welcome! What tidings bring'st thou? We have heard the growl of the crouched tiger; is his springing nigh?

Genevra: What of the strife? Shall we rejoice or weep?

Bernis: Rejoice for those who do their duty well. Weep for those whom this call may find not watching.

Constanza: Yes, but thy tidings first?

Bernis: The strife begins! Its issue brave hearts may not beat to know, but trusting ones may wait to learn.

Genevra: And what, what is the part for anxious love to do? Ah yes—to wait, to doubt, to hope, to dread—oh had I but a Lethe for my thoughts till I might know!

Constanza: And would'st thou too forget the poor forgotten prisoner? Would'st thou waste in cold oblivion the hours that wane so tedious on *his* watching? I would share in thought at least his grief, if I may not lighten its heaviness

Genevra: Oh dear Constanza! What shall I do? Teach me! But no, it were vain. Forgive me then; the wildness of my passion stops not to con its wish ere it be said.

Bernis: There is no need of passion, but of patience; there is no need of wildness, but of calm. Sister of Barri! Where is that proud spirit which marked your kindred best? Yields it to fear before thy brother's foes? He does not fear, should'st thou?

Genevra: Thou knowest me not—thou can'st not know, not having such a brother. But thou say'st that Barri fears not. True! The eagle's eye may look upon the Sun and quiver not, but is there other eye can follow it in its high gaze? My brother too may meet, unshaken, ay and proudly for himself a fate his sister

42

cannot think upon for him. There is a strength in the tried soul to bear its own companionless sufferings calmly, and clasp them to itself like blessings, but not another's! Could I change with him, thou would'st see if I shamed our kinsmanship! But speak not of patience or of calmness, 'tis not the time to hear thy homilies.

Bernis: But thou at least wilt hear.

Genevra: No! No! I'm deaf! Waste not thy arguments on me. Of what avail are they? Has argument the power to save my brother? If it has, oh haste, haste to restore him; but pause not to cast one word away on me! Alas! those sounds!

Bernis: Shrink'st thou to hear them? Dost thou then forget those are glad sounds to captives' ears, the watch-word to tell them that their friends are aiding them?

Genevra: Thou mean'st, to tell them that their friends *would* aid them.

Bernis: What? Must I even encounter thy distrust? Thou art a most suspicious proselyte.

Genevra: I *would* believe! And there are many too who would be atheists, but feel the force even while they speak of what they would deny. When I have clasped my brother to my heart, then I will laugh and call these idle fears, and trust another time.

Bernis: That other time! Deem'st thou that God may be more powerful? Or can'st thou not trust his power as confident now as another time?

Genevra: O chide me not! God will forgive. Thou dost not know my soul!

Enter Francoli.

Constanza: Thou here, Francoli? Com'st thou then to crush the last left hope? But no; thy looks are bright with happy tidings; share their happiness with us.

Francoli: Our cause will conquer! All is to thee madam, we owe, and thy reward is near. There is too much of good within our walls that impious feet should pass them.

Genevra: But how long before this game of life and death—this sport of butchers and their

44

prey, this slaughtering of what were once God's creatures till they chose to risk their name for what I dared to think and would not utter—ends?

Francoli: When we are victors; and have established by the only means by which we may, the freedom of our souls to use the powers which God has given them, according as the voice of God within may dictate. Would'st thou look upon the contest?

Genevra: Oh no! my heart's not mailed like your breast!

Constanza: But *I* would.

Genevra: Dear Constanza, do not go! Stay, stay with me; I cannot be alone.

Constanza: Well I will stay, so thou will be more calm. There is no further need for these wild fears, our cause is prosperous.

Francoli: Ay, prosperous. Who speaks of fear? Tis not the word for us! Nor time, nor place, nor cause that we should fear. Fear not! There is more strength in Bernis' words, which speak of Him who giveth strength, than all the arms and ordinance of ten thousand foes like these who league against but cannot—no they will not—overthrow us; and it is for Bernis that I come, if here his aid be not the most required.

Constanza: Oh no! We would not detain one citizen Leucate calls. We would not have one loyal soul inactive. Go Bernis, do thy part! 'Tis ours alas, to be unable to do aught but *feel*!

Francoli: Not so! 'Tis *thou* dost all.

Exuent Francoli and Bernis.

Constanza: Oh what is there in man—in civilized, high destined man, to whom the world were an inheritance too little for his hopes could it be given, because he grasps unnumbered worlds and bounds his flight beyond the stars—that he should stoop from the proud height to which his soul can soar to prove itself immortal? Stoop to crush a kindred soul, immortal like itself?

Genevra: *(interrupting)*: Ay, and my brother! That it is for *him* to be the sacrifice! There has a sad foreboding seized my soul which other days may prove; perhaps even this. 'Tis said such thoughts come but a little time before their warning be fulfilled.

Constanza: Thou'rt wild, Genevra. Thy words are passionate without a meaning.

Genevra: To my soul they have a fearful meaning!

Constanza: Oh Genevra, hush! These fears are idle; worse than idle, impious! Be thyself again— be Barri's sister and not the foolish thing thou seem'st now, dreaming whatever thy fancy dreams prophetic; would Barri own thee thus?

Genevra: Would Barri own me?! And it was thou, Constanza, spoke that word? Yes, Barri knows his sister better than thou, seem'st, to deem her heart as passionless as thine own high yet too unbending firmness! But do not mock my soul's deep oracle, nor call me foolish; for I cannot help believing what seems stamped and written here in such (it may be false—Oh, may it prove so!) in such seeming of reality. Oh, no! these thoughts are something more than idle. It cannot be that a mere dream should thus hang o'er my spirit with its misty fear, and still I try, and cannot shake it off!

Constanza: But dost thou try?

Genevra: No, not like thee, indeed! I do not speak of
               hopes and think despair. I cannot so disin-
               terest myself from all my former selfishness
               to be the patriot, not the sister, as thou
               can'st. And why, why should I try? Why
               should I hope? Thou tell'st me that our
               cause is prosperous, yet what is that to
               Barri? Do our enemies fail, will they then re-
               store the only prize which two months toil
               has gained? And do they win, then all is in
               their power; think'st thou that the vulture
               will relent because he finds his prey in-
               creased?

         (Constanza, who has been standing, sinks on a chair.)

               What have I said, Constanza? Oh could I
               but have thought! But heed me, not; I wan-
               der, rave.

Constanza: How could'st thou speak such things?
               Would thine own words prohibit every hope,
               even to thyself?

Genevra: Oh do not—do not heed me! Or make me too
               a prisoner if thou list, till I can learn to

prison such wild thoughts and keep them to myself.

Enter Hercules.

Hercules: Mamma, what ails thee? Shall I go ring the bell?

Constanza: No; stop, my love! Thy voice alone recovers me, sweet truster! Thou art so sure in thy simplicity, I cannot look on thee and doubt; I will not. Genevra, do not tempt my soul again.

Genevra: O leave me, leave me, let me rave alone!

Constanza: Not so! But I will try the power of song to soothe thy passion, not abandon thee to its wild sway; and though it fail in that, at least it will speed this heavy hour along. It is the song which Barri loved so well.
(Constanza sings):

Home! First and dearest spot!
    The young thoughts' boundary!
O can the wide world offer
    Another place like thee?
Where memory wreathes so fadeless
    Her fadeless evergreen?

And a charm is on the very air,
    To mark where joy has been?

Here sorrow finds a balm,
    And care a sweet relief—
And joy may blend its happiness
    With those who soothed its grief;
And here our hearts would linger,
    In thought of scenes gone by—
What are the world's wild dreams to this,
    The soul's first sanctu'ry!

O there are ties that bind us,
    To break too strong, too dear!
But the strongest and the dearest
    Are those which bind us here.
Home! 'tis a place of sunshine
    When all without is gloom;
The wide world cannot offer
    Another place like Home!

Enter Bernis.

Constanza: What say'st thou?

Bernis: That the righteous cause will prosper! The
    foe retreats. They cannot rally long; the city
    is our own!

Genevra: Whose is its *governor*?

Bernis: The city's! For they must deliver him to us
                 at last.

Constanza: Is that thy real thought?

Bernis: Most certainly. It is not of my order to trifle
                 ever—least at such a moment, and with
                 anxiety like thine; nor could I have a motive
                 that I should propose falsely to encourage
                 thee. It would but make truth more dreadful
                 when revealed.

Constanza: Then I will rest a moment more in confi-
                 dence; and try indeed, Genevra, to forget all
                 else in the one common thought! And now I
                 go to what my father loved to call his bower,
                 the old time-hallowed gallery where his
                 steps have left their traces; thence I may be-
                 hold the conflict, near as woman's nerves
                 might bear. Besides, I love to linger on that
                 spot. It is as though Cezelli were again re-
                 peating all the lessons he has taught in
                 other days, of fortitude and firmness; and
                 now indeed I need them!

                            Exit Constanza.

Genevra:	There, she's gone! The calm! The unmoved! Oh I would rather rave till I were mad indeed, than be like her.
Bernis:	Genevra, my profession pardons me for speaking to thee thus. I know thy grief. I've ever known thy brother worthy all the love thou givest him; yet I have spoke in accents of encouragement to thee, and I have tried to stimulate thy pride and to excite thy loyalty, in vain.
Genevra:	Say not in vain! But there are deeper feelings than pride, or loyalty, or transient hope, for me. A sister's love! What purer friendship? Can I be calm to think on that dear brother and know his fate uncertain? I *must* speak, else would the passion checked gush out within, and cause a wilder ruin there.
Bernis:	Then thou wilt place thy slightest case before the pang, the inward pang, which every word of thine wakes in another's heart. Her grief is not the less excessive that it is controlled. She would anticipate a brighter change but thy dark anticipations pall her hope, ere it be sure.

Genevra: Oh say no more! For her sake I will try to
              seem more calm.

Bernis: And may'st thou be supported in thine ef-
              fort, and *feel* the thing thou *seem'st*!

Genevra: That cannot be; but I will try.

Bernis: Then I again depart. Let not thy firmness
              vanish with my presence.

                        Exit Bernis.

Genevra: We too will seek some place, if such there
              be, where those harsh sounds may not in-
              trude so much.

              Exeunt Genevra and Hercules.

[As Scene III opens we find Barri in his prisoner's tent, frustrated that he is unable to join the battle he hears raging outside. Gerardo is carried in wounded, and Barri is dismissed to an inner part of the tent. Le Comte arrives. He and Gerardo discuss the turn the battle has taken against them. Le Comte is particularly galled that his army is being defeated by one led by a woman, and he vows to get revenge against both Constanza and Barri. Gerardo once again objects to Le Comte's plan, but then assents while remaining ambivalent. Barri is brought in and informed of Le Comte's intentions. - DLH]

Scene III: *The inside of a tent, guarded.*

Enter Barri, solus, pacing within.

Barri: My citizens are struggling in the strife, and I am here! That call is not for me! The voice of war unsheathes all swords but mine, and mine—where is it? In my jailor's keeping.

Enter a Guard.

How goes the contest, sir who tendest my cage? Waves my gay streamer freely, proudly yet?

Guard: Ay, but hands haste even now to pull it down.

Barri: Ah! Is that all? Well thou may'st go again, for my soliloquy no witness needs.

Guard: I go to witness nobler scenes than this!

                        Exit Guard.

Barri: *(Solus)*: Nobler indeed! But this tent is the bound to all *my* prospects; prisoned, guarded, watched—

                Again the battle's many varied tones break on my solitude with deep import of happiness or woe! But I must wait ere I may know the victors from the vanquished. Patiently wait! I am a prisoner!

                A prisoner, yes; I *am* a prisoner. I have a city yet at my command, but here my steps are fettered. I am wont to say to others—Go! Now others say to me—Remain! And I may not depart. I was a lord! This is my heritage. Man—man— how crooked is thy destiny. Thy web is woven with every changing tint that ever shaded joy or brightened grief. But this is not a time for quiet thought and calm reflection on the busy turns of man—that silk-worm! My mind shall contend with passions, though my body may not strive with outward foes.

(After a slight pause): Constanza has returned! There is one thing worthy my soul's best love. She heard the captive's cry and hastened back to loose the prisoned one! She saw my flag bend to the impious grasp of bloody hands and hastened back to rear it, free again! Oh I must rest in feebleness, and know my dearest ones unstrengthened by the might of love to mail this arm; beset by foes—a wall alone between them— and the spears of eager ruffians and their rosaries!

And my sweet, gentle boy! How bears *he* still this siege, unsheltered by a father's presence? Pales not the rose upon his faded cheek? Has not fear breathed too roughly on that form, sporting, till now, in luxury's choicest bowers? Bursts the young dimple out so merrily, to speak the laughing spirit of his soul? Does he sometimes forget, and utter—Father!—then weep to find no father answer him? Alas! He may not know that father's fate, too pure to think of ill; nor would I have his gay, young humor damped so hastily. My timid sister too! Oh *she* will know too well, and feel too sensibly this loss! She loves and fears and grieves to such excess, there is no middle place for her touched soul. And my Constanza! Hushed will be *her* grief, but not the less acute. I would it might be! Yes; for her sake, I would excuse awhile that she should hush a love which must be sorrow.

But these are tender thoughts; my soul must not yield to a softer mood than fits this place, this living sepulcher of warrior's fame. Yes I am buried here, my name effaced from Glory's brilliant record. Who will turn from all the illustrious names which grace her page to read the captive's humble signature, whose prison-barrier bounded his exploits? Eyes will pass lightly over, though hearts will stop, and sicken. But my spirit should be hardened, not melted by its ills. My soul is free, though here my form be penned! *That* shall exult in its proud consciousness of rectitude, and look upon its miseries as sports! My jailers shall not boast that *that* is bent! The tiger may be caged, but never tamed!

(Walks up and down the tent in silence a little space.)

(Shouts heard without.)

Again! Again! Oh God, defend thy cause! That is the shout to rally! Ah—they fail! The Leaguers fail! But for one instant now, when I might rush forth fiercer from this curb which has been put on me! Ah—would the fiends accomplish what they called a threat and give me indeed the choice with which they mocked my weakness, Leucate should not then have cause to blush that Barri was of her! And must that holy sanctuary be stained with its *own* life-stream? Sooner let the *scaffold*, that basest death and most inglorious, be stained with his who was its governor, and not a tear be shed to wash the stain.

The sounds approach! I can distinguish now voices amid the din—and nearer yet! And louder—even at my pavilion door!

Voices: Make way!

Guards: Back! Back! This is the prisoner's tent!

Barri.   Ah—they would help my memory to that
                name.

Voices.   Behold your chief! Close you the tent to
                him?

Guards.   Our chief? The Holy Virgin shelter him!

                Enter Soldiers, supporting Gerardo, wounded.

Barri.   Gerardo wounded? And his mournful look!
                The strife is ours—my city conquers still.
                And thus she sets a mark upon her foes.

Gerardo.   Bear me to yonder seat, for I must rest.

Soldier.   How may our services best aid thee further?

Gerardo.   Oh leave me now, and hasten to impart thy
                aid to those who need it more. My wound,
                my bodily wound, is slight—'tis a weakness
                only—fatigue—I cannot head you more to-
                day—but Le Comte wants your help. The
                wound is *here*, deep in my heart, which
                passes remedy. I could have died gladly, ex-
                ultingly, might I have seen that haughty
                banner low! But I must live, and see it wav-
                ing still in its proud loftiness, over my proud
                hopes.

59

Barri.	*(exclaims)*: 'Tis true! My banner floats triumphant still!
Gerardo.	Take him away! He is odious to my sight. What wounds my spirit most is balm to his; I will not see him joy, though silently, in what is cause for sadder mood to me.

Exit Barri, guarded, to an inner part of the tent.

Enter some Soldiers.

Soldier.	Yes! He is here indeed! Then all is lost! My hope failed not till now.
Gerardo.	Mine does not fail, and never shall! A soldier cannot fail in hope, and be a soldier still. And who is there that would belie that name? If there be such, let him no more mock with his coward breath the nobler fire he cannot imitate. Seek not my presence to insult me with your fears!
	But no—I wrong you, fellow soldiers; forgive my hastiness. But do not let your minds despond because the chance of war has turned a little while against us thus. I feel that I'm recovering rapidly.

Enter Le Comte.

Le Comte:	Art thou here in truth, Gerardo? The foe shall rue this ere my arm be stretched so weakly by my side.
	(To those around): Why do you not give him more prompt assistance?
Gerardo:	'Tis no need; faintness is all my hurt. I tried to scale, desperate, the wall; and something struck my head too rudely for the purpose. Here it is; 'tis a slight bruise, but on a tender place. They thought the task was done and bore me here before my dizziness was passed so far that I might bid them better use their strength. But is the contest ended for today?
Le Comte:	Methinks our prospects are not so inviting that we again should risk our bravest heads to strokes which might prove more than dizziness a second time.
Gerardo:	Ay, and our troops need respite to find again the courage they have lost. How stoutly all our efforts were resisted! This strife has been a shameful one for us, a noble one for

61

our antagonists. Bitterly, bitterly my pride feels the smart, sharper than all the wounds which ever tortured the feeblest frame.

Le Comte: Ay, and bethink thee, too, of what's more shameful still—of who has been this foe! A woman has out-generaled us. But yesterday we dreamt not of resistance; today, these paper walls have turned to iron. 'Tis well; there is an oft repeated proverb that pride must have a fall—and 'tis fulfilled, that's all.

Gerardo: It *is* not all, and shall not be! A soldier's pride shall not fall unavenged!

Le Comte: There is Gerardo's spirit! Here is mine to second it—and by our Holy League, *Revenge* shall be the third in fellowship! But is not this the prisoner's tent?

Gerardo: It is. Thy question was misplaced.

Le Comte: Forget'st thou then, our words before this strife began?

Gerardo: No! But I would forget them—all except the last. My memory needs no quickening. But sure thou would'st not now renew designs so useless? Barri is no longer Governor; let his perverseness irritate himself, but he is not an object to excite our anger or regard till deeper interests have been regarded first. 'Tis not on him we would revenge ourselves, but on Leucate; and not from passionate rage, but holy zeal.

Le Comte: Thou may'st be zealous, I will be revenged! I've sworn most sacredly; nor would, nor may, recall mine oath—and Barri, is he not the only instrument which we possess?

Gerardo: Which *thou* possess'st. Use not my name conjoint with such intents.

Le Comte: And has he not defied me? Dared me to make him arbiter between himself and what shall not be his again? Ay, thou hast heard him; but his empty vaunts shall not avert, but hasten—

Gerardo: Can'st thou doubt what would be Barri's choice? And knowing it, wilt thou, by making him a sacrifice, incense still more our foes and strengthen them with fury, where their fortitude might fail?

Le Comte: But 'tis not Barri who *shall* make the choice. He shall not be a self devoted martyr, for so their heretic blasphemy would term him. No! We will change our ordinance. It will be seen if she who keeps Leucate's keys so well will be as patriotic when the *cause* for which her selfishness turned patriotism is menaced. Ay, Constanza shall decide between her Barri and his—*our*—Leucate!

Gerardo: *(as if to himself)*: But 'tis not like a Spaniard to avail me of such advantage; to obtain from weakness what strength could not obtain.

Le Comte: And is it then more like a Spaniard to sit lonely thus, and let a woman shame, ay, conquer him? I ever heard it was a Spanish maxim, Eye for an Eye, Revenge for Injury—ever till now!

Gerardo: And now 'tis more than ever. Yes, let her choose; and if it be for Barri, Why then Leucate will be ours without the trouble of a further siege. And if she even can yield *him* to save the city, at least it will be her own free choice.

Le Comte: Think not that she can so belie her womanly nature; yet even though that were possible, we should but be as now we are.

Gerardo.	With this slight difference: we should be stained with innocent, noble blood! But why take I such interest in him? He's nought to me.
Le Comte.	Nought but an instrument for thy revenge!
Gerardo.	He is no instrument of mine. It is for thee alone to do with him as suits thee best.
Le Comte.	*(to the Guards).* Call Barri forth!

Exeunt Guards.

Now I will sound him to the very depth of his proud soul!

Enter Barri from the inner part of the tent, guarded.

Prisoner! I call thee here to bid thee be prepared for death; that is, if she who is to be thy judge decree it. Constanza is that judge, and 'tis with her to ransom thee and all thy citizens; you having first renounced your heresy by the surrender of Leucate's keys, and all the arms of its defenders, to us in the name of our most Holy League. But if that be refused, then she decrees thy death.

Leucate's Governor, or Leucate! That is the word!

And ho! Guards, soldiers there! See that a scaffold be erected, just before the wall, within ten paces thence.

Barri: *(Aside)*: Oh God! The measure of my shame is full! A scaffold! But 'tis better than a traitor!

Le Comte: And sound an armistice, and hasten! Hours are years in war's account.

              Exeunt Soldiers, Etc.

And prisoner, thou prepare thyself for thy swift pending fate of death—or life, a living death to all thy vaunted honor!

Barri: I'm prepared already! And thank thee that thou thus enablest me to die for that Immortal Cause which now my life no more may benefit. Have you further to speak with me? For I would pass my waning hours with God and with my soul, unbiased by men's converse, if I may.

Le Comte: Thou may'st!

Exit Barri.

Art thou recovered yet, Gerardo? Enough to
leave this place? For thou should'st be in a
more fitting quarter for thy rank.

Gerardo.   What is my rank in such a scene, which
equals all rank? But as thou choos'st. I am
recovered. 'Twas nothing but a bruise; a
paltry scratch! Lend me thine arm; see how
my strength returns! I will go undeceive the
one that gave a stroke so feeble, if he
deemed it harsh.

Exeunt omnes.

* * * * * * *

ACT III.

[In Scene I Constanza and Genevra learn that a scaffold has been built for Barri's execution. Bernis enters and tries to comfort them, asking them to trust in God's will. He then delivers the news that Constanza has the power to save her husband, but only if she will sacrifice the entire town in exchange. Constanza makes her choice, and prays to God for support. Francoli enters to tell her that she must announce her decision at sunset. - DLH]

Scene I. *Hall in the palace of Barri, as before.*

Enter Constanza, tearing a rose in pieces.

Constanza: When shall I clasp thee, Barri, once again to this lone heart, and hush the last faint doubts which linger still in sad rebellion here? Oh could I share captivity with thee! But that may not be. I will hasten then, its period with my hopes; for I *will* hope, till certainty be hopeless!

Enter Genevra and Hercules.

69

Hercules: Oh Mama! Thou hast torn my fairest rose!

Genevra: Ah! I have read the fairest flower will be the first to fade, the dearest friend will be the first to die.

Constanza: Thus ever all thou sayest terminates.

Genevra: Thus even all I think must terminate; my words are but the echo of my soul.

Constanza: But must they always echo to despair?

Genevra: Yes, when I *feel* it! Oh Constanza, had'st thou seen the thing which I have seen, thou woulds't not have asked that question! Had'st thou seen that scaffold! Oh God! My brain is giddy now!

Constanza: What said'st thou? What hast thou seen? A scaffold! Mean'st thou so? Or have thy fears but dreamt of such a thing?

Genevra: Ay, scaffold! Hercules should learn the name. His father's scaffold!

Enter Bernis.

70

Oh thou are come to read the sentence to us! Hasten! Quick, and banish every hope at once! It were better than to live on the very sport of hope.

Constanza: Oh speak!

Hercules: *(presenting Bernis a chair)*: Here is a chair.

Bernis: Bless thee, my child

Constanza: Oh father, bless me too! I need thy blessing.

Bernis: God blesses those whom he chastises most. We cannot tell his purpose, but we know his mercy, and in thankfulness should meet his heaviest chastisement.

Genevra: Then all is true! Oh I did hope till now!

Constanza: What? What is true? Speak out! There is no need of glossing over, with words of consolation, our despair. Is there a scaffold?

Bernis: Thou hast heard it then? That word is all. 'Tis but a slender choice; thy husband's honor, or his life, is doomed.

Constanza: His honor or his life! Oh God! My love! Then there is nothing left on earth for me. How could'st thou thus encourage? Bid me hope till hope seemed certainty, and I believed fondly that all was certain, but to crush my soul the heavier now? (*Falls fainting.*)

Hercules: Help—help mama! Look! She is dying! Aunt Genevra! Bernis! Will you not come to her?

Constanza: Oh could I die indeed!

Bernis: Thy time has not yet come. Thy cup over-flows not yet with all the bitterness which earth must add to it ere thou may'st taste the last.

Genevra: I thought till now my heart would break; yet I live on and hear my gloomiest fears verified. What new power has strengthened me? But 'tis not true. 'Tis all a scheme, a feint; they dare not harm one hair on Barri's head! Who said there was a scaffold? 'Tis all false. Bernis would frighten me, because I heed not his cold admonishments, and cannot learn to be as calm and tranquil as Constanza.

Constanza:	As calm! And have I then been calm for this? Yet I am calm; I do not rave. Oh here, here is the conflict! Here my tears are checked and frozen; how they press upon my heart! Oh might they flow and bear my life-stream too!
	(To Bernis): But did'st thou say my cup was not yet filled with all its bitterness? That cannot be. His honor or his life! I know the choice Barri will make.
Bernis:	What were Constanza's choice?
Constanza:	Father! I thank thee that this draught is spared! I could not choose, for Barri might not be without his honor; and could I decree mine own, my son's, Genevra's, wretchedness, for a mere name?
Bernis:	And could'st thou then decree thine own, thy son's, Genevra's, *Barri's* shame, for mere existence?
Constanza:	Would'st thou torture me? Or is my misery to be doubled yet? If thou hast any sharper pang to add, spare not—tell all at once. But speak, Oh speak! Despair loves to hear over and over its tale.

Bernis: I have indeed a sharper pang to add, but this will give the fortitude to bear it. *(holding up a Bible.)*

Constanza: Oh do not think but I can bear it all! I can bear anything but not to know what I must bear!

Bernis: Then—thine must be the choice. The city or its Governor. They have said that thou should'st choose between them. Yield the one, or by denial doom the other's death.

Genevra: Ah! Is there any chance? Can he be saved?

Bernis: The city is his ransom. All the lives of these brave citizens are forfeited, or his. One life for all, or all for one.

Genevra: And dost thou hesitate to choose, Constanza?

Constanza: I cannot! They have mocked me with a choice which is not mine! As though it were for me to balance destinies and make myself an arbiter of life, who would resign my own with joy! I cannot hesitate; but oh my voice can never utter it. Speak for me! Thou art gifted to express thy grief in words; what were *thy* choice, Genevra?

Genevra: My choice! Oh were the world to be his ransom, and had I worlds to give, how easily my choice were made!

Bernis: And would'st thou sacrifice the world for one? Others can love as purely as thou dost, and as strong, though not—

Genevra: So selfish. I know what thou would'st say, yet 'tis not all my selfishness. And might the universe be pledged indeed for him, there were not found a soul more noble to redeem the pledge. And here in this faint city, which has shrunk to meet the conflict till Constanza came, nothing is worth the half of Barri's life. Ay, call me selfish! But it is not that—'tis the close tie which ever knit our hearts from their twin growth, in twin-ness of affection, which makes me place his life before all else—or place *my* life for his! For I would die, willingly, joyfully, but to know he lived! And is that selfishness?

Constanza: My God—I know that thou art merciful! And oh, I feel that thou art inscrutable. But till this proof, I ever thought the consciousness

75

of doing right would balance every grief that sacrifice of present joy might cause.

Bernis: And think so still! Thy thoughts are passionate now, and quick and changing; but when thou art calm and quiet in thy suffering, thou wilt find that inward approbation will repay the sacrifice of every selfish hope to duty, and to honor, and to God. Thou can'st not doubt what Barri's choice would be; then can thine own be wavering?

Constanza: Oh no! I cannot doubt of Barri's choice, and mine were made as readily were I the victim! 'Tis easier to suffer all the woes of others than to add one pang to them; to be oneself the only sacrifice than to condemn another to endure the slightest, swiftest pain. Oh! Did I say condemn? Oh that I could condemn all hope of other earthly pleasure to myself, so that were *all* my judgment might affect! And shall Constanza's hand seal Barri's fate? And shall her voice pronounce it? Oh that word would be the last! Ay *(to Bernis)* look reproof at me, thou dost not know how hard a thing it is to part with all the soul holds dear on earth, even though returned to heaven! But oh, I feel—no! no— I do not feel; it passes feeling!

Bernis: Did not the patriarch give his only son to
             God, who asked him? Did not God too give
             His son to be a ransom for the world? 'Tis
             His cause in which we struggle now, and 'tis
             to Him this sacrifice is given!

Constanza: Yes, yes, I know; I know my fearful task.
             Thou who hast willed, support me to per-
             form it! But leave me now, all leave me!
             Thou, my child—my child! Yes thou art still
             mine own! Their power could not extend to
             thee; but go, my love. And thou too, my sis-
             ter. Ah we are indeed sisters in sorrow as in
             kinsmanship; oh leave me too. I must not
             hear thy voice nor listen to thine eloquence
             of woe. Thou must not make me weaker
             than I am, nor wake my senses from the
             fearful trance which will not let me realize
             my loss. And Bernis, thou too go a little
             space, for I would be alone in wretchedness.

Bernis: I go; but to thy care I first entrust this pledge
             from God to man. I give it thee to be thy con-
             solation and thy guide. *(giving her the Bi-
             ble.)*

             Thou will be rewarded for thy struggle at
             last, and Barri will approve thee.

77

Constanza: Now thou'st touched the string which vibrates.

Genevra: I depart to seek in solitude more sure despair, where once I loved to go and seek relief from my almost satiety of bliss in other, happier, un-returning days. The foxes have their holes, the birds their nests; Genevra hath not where to lean her heart in this wide world and not be shaken off. Come boy! All places are alike henceforth to me and misery, my future twin.

           Exeunt Genevra, Bernis, and Hercules.

Constanza: *(sola.)* They're gone! And this is left to counsel me. *Here*, at least, I may find consolation! (*opens at this passage*): "Blessed are they that mourn, for I will be their comforter."

           And be thou mine, Oh God! Yes, I will come to thee and seek that rest thou promises to all who seek it thus. *(she kneels.)*

           Oh Thou to whom the sorrowful may come and tell their sorrows, Thou who knowest my soul, and knowest how purely, truly it has loved, 'Thy will be done!' Oh teach thy supplicant, who kneels before thee in her lowliness, to love *thy* pleasure though it be *her* grief. My spirit shrinks! Oh God! I know the part which I must do—Support my weak resolve! Thou call'st me to resign what thou hast given; have I loved the gift too well to think of thee, the Giver, as I ought? But now the dream is past—I wake to earth again. 'Twas a vision of such ecstasy! My God! I thank thee for it. Yet 'tis right that Thou should'st take it from me, for it bound my love too much to earth to think of Heaven. But must *I* be the one to speak his fate? I, who would die for him, to cause *his* death? Father, forgive me if my soul revolts to make its dreadful choice! But it *is* made. Put—put an iron firmness in my heart till all is over, and then, oh might it break! *(she rises.)*

I have resolved. My purpose shall not shake. No! No. 'Tis fixed; irrevocably fixed. I have done right; but all the agony of guilt is tearing me! Yet it was right. Oh Barri! When we parted in this hall one little moon ago who could have thought we parted then forever, or to meet only again in such a scene—the last! Where I should be the judge, and thou the doomed!

Yet I might save thee. No—it were an insult to thine high spirit. I *might* save my love, but *Barri*, never. I should but preserve thee a little while to see thee waste away slowly, and lingeringly, and broken hearted.

Traitor or patriot! Do I hesitate to choose the name for Barri? But my boy—oh may he live to thank me for depriving his childhood of its guardian, rather than deprive his manhood of its dignity or rob his father of a warrior's name. Yes, I am fixed. No power shall shake me now, save His who has decreed this trial to me.

Enter Francoli.

Francoli: I have been sent to—to—

Constanza: Ah, well I know thy message. 'Tis no need that I should hear those fiendish words again.

Francoli: I would not speak then. At sunset thou wilt choose. Our Holy Cause aid thee!

Constanza: At sunset did'st thou say? So soon? Well it is better so than that my purpose should

waver in its lingering to be done. At sunset
I shall be alone on earth!

Francoli: Oh say not so! Thou wilt have fellowship in
grief at least. But we will wear the willow rather than tear the laurel from his brows.

Constanza: I thank thee for thy words; they strengthen
me. I would remember nothing now but
Barri the *warrior*, not the friend. But let me
go and breathe my—sentence—in the open
air, lest it should be stifled ere confirmed.

Exeunt Constanza and Francoli.

*[This final scene finds all preparations made for Barri's ex-
ecution. The scaffold is ready, the prisoner is brought
forth, and those within the palace arrive to deliver the decision and witness the execution. – DLH.]*

Scene II. *On the rampart of Leucate and the plain below.*
A scaffold just before the wall,
sun seen not far above the horizon.

Enter on the plain Gerardo leaning on Le Comte,
Barri, and Guards.

Le Comte: *(to Barri)*: Behold thy death-couch! Or thou
              shalt behold a wider wreck in yonder teem-
              ing herd. Thou hast but one alternative: to
              die the death before thee, or to live and be a
              by-word, a reproach, a shame to life. Ay, we
              have said it; who shall dare unsay? Le
              Comte has marked thee for his vengeance;
              who shall rescue thee? Yon sun which wan-
              eth now to close thy life, or tarnish its bright
              fame, shall never rise for thee again, or rise
              but to behold thy brand forever fixed.

Gerardo: Hush! It is not a hero's part to mock the
              fallen with their wo!

Barri.   I am content to bear thy words. They but reprove thyself, and cannot mar the inward consciousness of my own soul's approval.

Le Comte.   Shall I never, not even in this last effort, humble thee, thou insect in my path?

Barri.   It is not thus, nor by such efforts, thou may'st humble me. But thou hast bound me in thy gratitude (which I may not leave unexpressed) by this regard to my last pleasure, here to place before the very wall which I redeem, this sign of its redemption; *here* to grant that I may breathe my soul out in the arms, almost, of those for whom 'twas sweet to live, for whom 'tis sweet to die.

                 (ascending the scaffold): My part is done. My goal is reached! I stand in triumph here. Yes, it is triumph thus to guard my trust even to the scaffold. What is in that name that I should dread to have it linked with mine? It cannot brand me at the higher bar to which I hasten, nor can it ever blot my memory from fond hearts I leave behind. 'Tis but its union with the perjured names of those who did what I die to avoid that makes it infamous. The warrior dreads not

a warrior's death, and is not martyrdom more glorious than that?

Le Comte: Hold! Not so fast! There is another to pronounce thy fate, ere it be sure. Thy foot may yet retrace its path to earth again, and thou may'st clasp thy dearest, who contemns all trusts for thee, once more to thy freed heart.

Barri: No—never! Never! I will not live to see my faith betrayed. I will not clasp dishonor to my heart, nor pass to earth again to be a stain on its fair surface. Here I stand to die!

Le Comte: Die then! But do not burst with thy big purpose before thou may'st fulfill it. Thou would'st lose the glory then of dying for thy cause by dying for thy temper. But they come! The Angel of Deliverance is nigh! Now, thou who art so prodigal of life, pause till the voice of love restore its power.

Enter on the rampart Constanza and Francoli.

Barri: *(Aside):* Yes; they come. *She* comes! Mine own Constanza! Comes to redeem my honor, comes to be her husband's judge! And must I take farewell of that

dear one forever? Death, I thought thy
bitterness was past.

Constanza: *(leaning on Francoli)*: Oh now it comes with
its full force upon me! I was stunned, bewil-
dered, stupefied before; oh God! God support me through my fearful task!

Le Comte: *(addressing Constanza)*: A warrior's saluta-
tion welcomes thee! We sheathe our swords
and wait for thee to say if we again shall
draw them here. Thou'st heard our message; 'tis thy part then to surrender thy city
on our terms, or him who was its Governor
on what terms thou see'st by still preserving
that. We ask thy choice between them.

Barri: Oh let Cezelli's daughter make the choice
Cezelli would approve, or Barri dictate. Forget our love! Yes now forget even that! Think
but of Barri's honor; be not thou the one to
set the seal upon its fall. Do not betray my
trust even for my life! What is a traitor's life?
And that were mine should'st thou—

Le Comte: 'Tis not for thee to guide her choice! Let it be
free, uninfluenced, her own.

Constanza: *(to Francoli)*: His words restore my firm-
                ness. I knew he was mine own, my noble
                Barri still!

Gerardo: Let not the sun set on thy hesitation!

Constanza: I do not hesitate! My choice is made but I
                would find the words to utter it. Oh cannot
                I die? May not *my* life fill the measure of
                your stern barbarity? My fortune, my life,
                accept; for they are mine! And willingly, God
                knows how willingly, I would resign them for
                his sake. Ay, thank your clemency which
                would receive them from me! But must I
                choose? And is there no reprieve?

Le Comte: We asked thy choice alone, on *our* condi-
                tions.

Constanza: Then that choice is made. All that is *mine* I
                give to ransom him; but the city is the
                King's—my honor, God's! Not even for Barri
                may I forfeit them.

Gerardo: Thou hast chosen nobly. Yet we give thee
                space still further to reflect, ere thou shalt
                say the final word which may not be re-
                called.

Constanza: I've said it! Are the words so pleasant to you that you would hear them over again?

Le Comte: We wait for softer humor to revoke their sternness.

Barri: Monster! Unfeeling! Waste thy taunts on me! Mock not at her, because her soul *can* feel and thine is *senseless!*

Le Comte: Does the victim's cry stay the raised knife that wavers over it?

Gerardo: Le Comte! I blush for thee; restrain thy speech! Is death a merriment that thou should'st sport with those who stand the nearest on its brink?

Le Comte: Only from thee would I endure such show of sovereignty, nor always even from thee. Break thou our league and I will break our friendship. I am not tamely bound to bear thine insults, because 'tis thou insultest.

Gerardo: Nay, thou hast wronged me; do not mistake equality for pride. I would not break our league nor mar our friendship, nor would I make my friendship less for thee by suffering faults where I might teach improvement.

Le Comte:	Thou art intolerable! But we will speak another time of this. Now let us haste to bring the crisis on—of life, or death.
Gerardo:	But 'tis not sunset yet.
Le Comte:	Right, she may play till then the patriot. She may yet retain her lion's skin. That moment will unmask her.

Enter Hercules on the rampart, running to Constanza.

Constanza:	My child! My fatherless child, art thou too come to see thy father die? But linger not in such a place my boy, lest thy pure blood congeal and pause in ice-drops at its source. The veil must not be lifted to unfold such sights as thy young soul never dreamt of yet. Trust still that earth is fair! Too soon, alas, it will darken at thy gaze.
Barri:	*(Aside)*: My son! My son—my little orphan boy! Oh it is hard to leave this clinging earth, too sweet, alas, with all its bitterness. Hard, did I murmur? It is thy will, Oh God; then it be mine!

Le Comte: Time wanes; perhaps thy firmness now may
               fail! If so, thou may'st even yet recall thine
               answer, for we would not have thee war
               against thy nature. And if tears are signs of
               its returning power, thy second thought
               may prove indeed less patriotic, but more
               like a wife's, a woman's, and a mother's.

Constanza: Thou dost mistake me then! My answer's
               made; or choice, or judgment, or whatever
               name you give to that which had no need till
               now of any, and I do not sport with words.
               'Tis Barri's choice, 'tis honor's choice, and
               mine! It must not be recalled. I know my
               heart may break but it would still retain
               that purpose with its last gasp.

Francoli: But let me urge thee now, to seek some rest
               from grief. The sun declines; thou hast en-
               dured too much already; more thou may'st
               not bear. Thy soul is tired with anguish. Let
               me support thy steps, but linger not!

Constanza: Shall I desert his death-bed? Yes that is his
               death-bed, though a scaffold. I will watch till
               all is over. This comfort shall be his, to know
               at least his friends look on him when more
               they may not do.

Barri.	Oh this is bliss indeed, to see thee to the last! But thou can'st not endure the shock, the rush from life to death. No! No; thou must let me die alone, unpitied and un-moved.
Gerardo.	And we must tear such nobleness from earth?
Le Comte.	Thou hast said we must, or strip its lofty character.

Enter Genevra on the rampart.

Genevra:	Then all is lost indeed! Constanza! Oh, where shall I turn? My brother—do I see thee thus, like a guilty thing? And thou art doomed, and I have now no brother!
Barri.	Do not mourn my gentle sister, for I do not mourn to die for those I love, when I could live only to be an infamy to them.
Genevra:	An infamy? A blessing! Thou hast been a thing for me to twine my soul around, and live but in the embrace! Yet can I not die, though I would, with thee.

Ye iron men, whose armor is your emblem, if there be one spark of mercy left within your breasts, oh change the victim—let *me* die for him!

Barri: Genevra! Be my sister still! I die, I must. There is no chance or wish remaining that I should live. I die in honor's cause, and willingly. Let not thy pleading change me! Do not regret me thus, but think of me, when I am gone, as of a happy spirit which hovers near thee till it may recall its loved ones to it in that blessed sphere where friends part not, and malice may not come. Till then farewell, my sister! Do not weep for me, but joy that I may die at last for that which my *life* has failed to benefit.

Genevra: My brother! Oh my brother, speak not thus! Say not farewell! Oh say it not! 'Twill be enough to know the dreadful certainty without this quiet parting.

Enter on the rampart Bernis and Citizens.

Ah! Thou hast come, Bernis, and thou, and thou, brave citizens! Come to behold your Governor sacrificed; a pleasant spectacle, and well attended! What is your fee, my chiefs, for such a sight?

Le Comte: Lady, had'st thou not better seek a place more fitting for thy words? Thy grief has lost the balance of discretion.

Genevra: Yes, I know that I am wild! It is strange I should be! There is no cause, not any, for such passion! I come to see my brother die, that's all! I've seen him live, but that is ended now. And I would trespass on your courtesy for this last sight of him. My gallant friends, look well and measure by his *nobleness* your own degeneracy!

Citizen: Oh might my blood be shed for his, it should revoke those words.

Genevra: It cannot be, so thou may'st safely boast.

Citizens: *(various)*: Boast? 'Tis not boasting!

By his blood I swear that mine should be the first to flow for him! Ay, and it shall be, fellow citizens!

Stand we thus tamely to behold him die who should stand first among us?

One bold stroke and all is ours and Barri is restored. Who's here adventurous enough to second my words with deeds? Who would the readiest prove his patriotism, his loyalty, his valor? Let him stand forth and join me!

Sound the alarm!

The Drum!

The Drum!

Ho—to the rescue all!

To Barri's rescue!

Strike!

The day's our own!

Constanza: His rescue! Oh my God! My soul was nerved against every misery, but not for this. This weight of *joy*—it is too much. Support me!

Francoli: Had'st thou but gone before!

Bernis: Ye madmen, pause! Touch not your arms! Is it thus you'd sacrifice Leucate too, with Barri? For it were vain to speak of rescuing him with such a band. Look to the foe! They're armed, prepared. The guards have closed round him.

Citizens: Let them be prepared!

              We are resolved!

Bernis: Resolved for what? To break your word, your faith, given in a soldier's name? Who is there here so traitorous to his honor, so traitorous to his cause? Let him stand forth and abdicate all claims henceforth to rights he would annihilate by his example!

Besiegers: *(Shout)*: Come on! Come on! We'll give you welcoming!

Genevra: What have I caused? What have I done?

Le Comte: *(to besiegers)*: Peace! Peace!

              It is from you—Leucate's chiefs, I ask an explanation. What are we to deem from this? Do you decline to keep engagements with your foes? Or know you not the practices of War?

Bernis: Ask not of us! We keep engagements, but we cannot keep men's passions always bridled at out will. 'Twas but a sudden swell, a passing gust, a flash, like summer lightning, leaving all as tranquil as before.

But hasten now before the thunder gathers to complete what must be done!

Gerardo: Then we once more permit the lady to declare if still her choice be firm.

Constanza: Firm! Firm. Am I not firm? (Francoli, do not withdraw thine arm; I have not quite recovered from)—Yes, it is firm; ask not again that horrid question.

Gerardo: Guards, then stand off from the prisoner. Let him speak, if aught he has to say to those who fain would hear.

Le Comte: We want no dying speeches!

Gerardo: Thou can'st not deny this only privilege to one who, I dare pledge myself, will not betray it.

Genevra:	Oh then my time has come! And have I lived to see this hour?
Hercules:	Mamma! Mamma!
Constanza:	My child! Turn not thine eyes that way. Oh I am faint!
Francoli:	Had'st thou not better go, even now?
Constanza:	Go? Where? Away from Barri at this latest hour, when most my love is proved? Oh no! Seek not again to move my purpose. I will never leave him in life, nor can death long divide us. 'Tis sweet to breathe the air he breathes, to catch the breeze which wafts his parting sigh to me. But hark! He speaks! That voice! Thine arm again!
Barri:	My fellow citizens! Ye who have been ever the strong in hand and brave in heart, he who was once of you would now express his hearty thanks for all your services while yet he may. Our path has ever been, till now, together; but the parting comes. Yours, fellow-citizens, I know will be, as it has been before, a glorious one. *My* course must cease on earth. Oh God! Resume its thread

where earthly passions cannot come to sever it again!

To you, Defenders of what was once my city and my home, but cannot now be even my grave—I leave all my soul most has loved: my wife, my child, my sister, friends, companions of that life which now has reached its limit. In my name, protect them and defend them! Be their guard from every ill! And when you speak of me, speak not with pity, fellow-citizens, for my untimely, unexpected fate; I should more need your pity if I lived, but now I need it not—I wish it not! My nearer, dearer, most familiar friends, Farewell!

Constanza! Oh I thank thy choice, even with my dying words! And I would speak of many things to thee, my love. But now that were but aggravation, for thou know'st well, all that I would say; and well I know all thou would'st answer. Let that pass; my soul has little more to do with words of earth.

Genevra, weep not thus! Mourn not for me as one to be regretted, or deplored. Have I not said that death is sweet to me, in such a cause? Only 'tis bitterness to see my dearest weep, when I could joy but for their tears!

But I will not be long. My words refuse their office. I had wished, could I have lived with honor, to have seen my son the pride and glory of my years. I too had other dreams, even of myself; and brilliant hopes of fame; but they are past! All, all is past, and earth is passing from me, and I shall pass from earth; yet there are hearts I shall not pass from. But I would not have my memory there be sorrowful, but sweet. I will pray, thus leaning over the grave, for those loved ones! Be theirs a happier fate!

Father! be thou the father of my child, and lead him through life's wildering maze, still thine! Be thou also *her* father! Be thy holy word her consolation and her happiness. And never let a murmur, though unsaid, find echo in her farthest soul for this. Genevra, too; for all, for all, I pray, my friends and foes, they are alike to one who stands before his Maker.

If my soul has ever been too quick to take offence, too tardy to forgive it, now 'tis past. Once more, my friends, farewell! God! in thy hands I leave them, for their trust is in thy power, and to *that* power I yield submissively; not to the might of man.

Farewell! Farewell, sister, and wife, and child! Oh think of me, but not with sorrow. Citizens, farewell! And I would gaze once more upon those towers where I have often lingered at this hour. Adieu, dear native scenes! I gaze on ye for the last time!

And thou, bright Sun! yet stop till I have taken my last fond look of earth; tonight we go together, thou, to rise again, and light some other to his grave—I to the world of Suns that *never* set. Thou art gone! I must not linger. Executioner! I'm ready! Do thy part! My hour has come. Oh earth and earthly happiness, farewell! Heaven, pardon and accept my guilt-stained soul!

Le Comte: *(to the Executioner)*: Strike not! Strike not!

(to Constanza): Lady; thou yet may'st save him; one word from thee!

Constanza: Oh God! Thou'rt merciful! Three times my word has doomed him! Said he not himself that he was ready? So am I! Be done! Be done! Seek not from agony what calmer grief denied!

Gerardo: Then strike!

Constanza: Oh Barri! *(she faints)*

Hercules: Papa! That sword! That sword!

Bernis: Boy, come away!

Genevra: *(rushing towards the barricade)* Hold me not! Hold me not! I will die with him!

Francoli: *(grasping her)* Cease, cease, for his sake, cease!
                (Genevra falls fainting upon the rampart.)

Le Comte: *(to the Executioner)*: Why loiterest thou, Man, in thine office?

Executioner: Did'st thou bid me strike?

Le Comte: Yes, sirrah! Strike! Or thine own head's the forfeit!

Executioner: Then God bear witness to my innocence! His blood be on *thy* hands, not mine!

Le Comte: Fool, strike, and parley not!

Bernis: Vengeance awaits the proud!

Francoli: Glory the martyred! Ah, that drum—'tis well! He has at least a soldier's requiem.

Citizens: And soldiers' prayers!

                Long live the memory of our noble Governor, while the walls he ransomed shall remain!

                Long live Leucate!

                Long live Leucate!

                Vengeance to her foes!
                Drums sound, bells of Leucate toll, Citizens shout, &c.

www.ingramcontent.com/pod-product-compliance
Lightning Source LLC
Chambersburg PA
CBHW061254170626
46809CB00007B/2995